Grub's pups

For Mum and Dad with love A.B.

For Lee S.W.

First published in Great Britain in 2011
This edition published 2015
Deepdene Lodge, Deepdene Avenue,
Dorking, Surrey, RH5 4AT, UK
www.bonnierpublishing.com

Text copyright © Abi Burlingham, 2011
Illustrations copyright © Sarah Warburton, 2011

Printed and bound in China

ISBN: 978 1 84812 508 7 (paperback)

1 3 5 7 9 10 8 6 4 2

Grub's Pups

Abi Burlingham
Illustrated by Sarah Warburton

PICCADILLY PRESS • LONDON

This is me.

I'm Ruby.

This is Grub.

A very exciting thing is going to happen –
Grub's going to be a dad!

Can you believe it?

I can't,

Joe can't,

and Grub definitely can't!

Grub wants to play with Tilly
but Tilly doesn't want to play.

"It's all right for you, Grub," I say.

"At least you haven't got a tummy full of pups."

But Tilly has.

Tilly is enormous!

Billy and I are having a
Guess how many pups competition.
I guess five.
Billy guesses ten.

Billy's mum says, if it's that many,
they will have to move house.

Tilly seems restless.

I think she is finding the very exciting thing
very un-exciting!

It's the Grublets. They are making Tilly tired.

Grub doesn't understand.

He gives Tilly his paw and makes snuffly noises.

But Tilly isn't interested.

She just flops on her side in the shade.

I found Grub under my bed,
snuggled up to Fluff and Snooky and Plod.
I think he's lonely.
I think he's missing his cuddles and
playtime with Tilly.

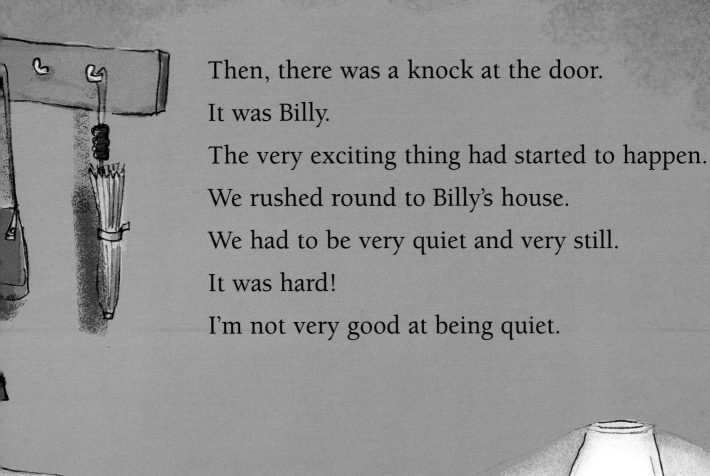

Then, there was a knock at the door.

It was Billy.

The very exciting thing had started to happen.

We rushed round to Billy's house.

We had to be very quiet and very still.

It was hard!

I'm not very good at being quiet.

Then the puppies started
to appear.

"One!" said Billy's mum.

"Two!" said Billy's mum.

"Three!" squealed Billy's mum.

We waited
and waited
and waited . . .

. . . but nothing happened,
so we had some strawberry milkshake and ice cream.

Those three Grublets were
the thirstiest puppies ever!

Then suddenly . . .

"Four!" shouted Billy's mum.

Four little Grublets, all squeaky
and wriggly!

"Five!" squealed Billy's mum.

"Look! Something's wrong," said Billy.

The fifth little Grublet wasn't squeaking at all.

Billy's dad picked up the fifth little Grublet
and rubbed and rubbed and rubbed.
Finally, the fifth little Grublet started to wriggle and sniffle,
and then he let out the tiniest little "Squeak".

"Hooray!" we cheered.

Joe came to see the Grublets too.

That was when I realised –

I'm champion of the *Guess how many pups* competition.

Hooray!

Grub is not impressed.

He keeps trying to get Tilly's attention,

but Tilly is busy with her babies.

"She's a mum now," I tell Grub.

"She doesn't want to play."

The Grublets keep getting

bigger and bigger and bigger.

"Number one looks like Tilly," said Billy. "Let's call her Rosie."

"Number five looks like Grub," I said. "Let's call him Squeak."

We want to keep them all.

I don't think Grub wants us to keep any of them.

Grub just wants Tilly back.

He keeps moping and huffing and puffing.

The next morning, Tilly leapt up from the puppies and ran outside.

I think she could hear Grub in the garden.
She has very good ears.

She started woofing for Grub!